Monday Monday Monday
Monday Monday Monday
Monday Monday Monday

Tuesday Tuesday Tuesday
Tuesday Tuesday Tuesday
Tuesday Tuesday Tuesday
Tuesday Tuesday Tuesday

Wednesday Wednesday
Wednesday Wednesday
Wednesday Wednesday
Wednesday

Thursday Thursday Thursday
Thursday Thursday
Thursday Thursday Thursday

Friday Friday Friday Friday
Friday Friday Friday Friday
Friday Friday Friday Friday

Saturday Saturday
Saturday Saturday Saturday
Saturday Saturday
Saturday Saturday

Sunday Sunday Sunday
Sunday Sunday Sunday Sunday
Sunday Sunday Sunday

Monday
Monday Monday Monday
Monday Monday
Monday Monday Monday

Tuesday Tuesday
Tuesday Tuesday Tuesday Tuesday
Tuesday Tuesday
Tuesday Tuesday

Wednesday
Wednesday Wednesday
Wednesday Wednesday Wednesday
Wednesday

Thursday Thursday Thursday
Thursday Thursday
Thursday Thursday Thursday

Friday Friday Friday Friday
Friday Friday Friday Friday
Friday Friday Friday Friday

Saturday Saturday
Saturday Saturday Saturday
Saturday Saturday
Saturday Saturday

Sunday Sunday Sunday
Sunday Sunday Sunday Sunday
Sunday Sunday Sunday

SCRATCHES AND SCRAPES

By Margo Linn ■ Illustrated by Doreen Gay-Kassel

SCHOLASTIC INC.

New York Toronto London Auckland Sydney Mexico City New Delhi Hong Kong

For Jennifer Hochhauser

ISBN 0-439-23225-2
Text copyright © 2000 by Margo Linn.
Illustrations copyright © 2000 by Doreen Gay-Kassel.

12 11 10 9 8 7 6 5 4 3 2 1   1 2 3 4 5/0
Printed in China for PUBLISHING PARTNERS.
Bandages made in Japan
First Scholastic printing, December 2000.

Alexander P. Yam got bruises and bumps.
Scrapes on his elbows; scratches and lumps.

Then he would cry,
   or whine, or wail.
A bandage would comfort him,
   always...

without fail!

On Monday Alexander got
a scrape on his knee.
He put on three bandages,
which are easy to see.

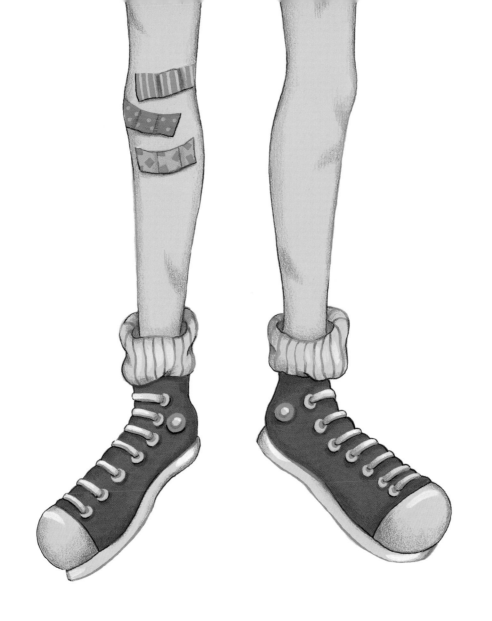

On Tuesday's hike
  Alex tripped and fell down.
"Just one bandage today,"
  said Mom with a frown.

A sneeze,

a cough,

a hiccup,

a choke...

Alex thinks a bandage works better than a COKE®!

On Wednesday Alexander was stung by a bee.
He cried until someone bandaged his knee.

On Thursday his brother said,
"Alexander, you pip!

You can't eat ice cream
if you bandage your lip!"

On Friday his sister said, "Alex, me too!

I want pretty bandages just like you."

On Saturday Alex got
a big, red blister.

Who gave him a bandage?
His nice little sister!

A big bandage to cover a scab that was ugly,

Left Alex feeling happy and all warm and snuggly.

On Sunday there were no new bumps or bruises.

But Alex had bandages from his head to his shoeses.

Alexander took a long bath;
all the bandages came free.

Alexander was clean
    and smooth as could be.

On Monday Alex's cowboy
fell out of a tree.
Alex made him better
by bandaging his knee.

Then Alexander P. Yam rolled down a steep hill.
He had scratches all over and cried until....

Monday Monday Monday
Monday Monday Monday
Monday Monday

Tuesday Tuesday Tuesday
Tuesday Tuesday Tuesday
Tuesday Tuesday Tuesday
Tuesday Tuesday

Wednesday Wednesday
Wednesday Wednesday
Wednesday Wednesday
Wednesday

Thursday Thursday Thursday
Thursday Thursday
Thursday Thursday Thursday

Friday Friday Friday Friday
Friday Friday Friday Friday
Friday Friday Friday Friday

Saturday Saturday
Saturday Saturday Saturday
Saturday Saturday
Saturday Saturday

Sunday Sunday Sunday
Sunday Sunday Sunday Sunday
Sunday Sunday Sunday

Monday Monday Monday
Monday Monday Monday
Monday Monday Monday

Tuesday Tuesday Tuesday
Tuesday Tuesday Tuesday
Tuesday Tuesday Tuesday

Wednesday Wednesday
Wednesday Wednesday
Wednesday Wednesday
Wednesday

Thursday Thursday Thursday
Thursday Thursday
Thursday Thursday Thursday

Friday Friday Friday Friday
Friday Friday Friday Friday
Friday Friday Friday Friday

Saturday Saturday
Saturday Saturday Saturday
Saturday Saturday Saturday
Saturday

Sunday Sunday Sunday
Sunday Sunday Sunday Sunday
Sunday Sunday Sunday